FIREMAN'S CLAIM

A BBW Alpha Male Romance

Jolie Damman

CONTENTS

CHAPTER 1

Leana

I thought that my life was going to take a different turn. But, here I was, in my apartment, looking out the window and drinking my life away. Nothing was going to change. I was a model, and things were going well in the money department, but that still didn't mean I loved my life.

I needed something else.

Something that could make me look at all this, all this fame and the city beyond, and make me think that I was taking the right path.

My hand was holding a wine glass. It was made of the finest kind of glass in the whole country, and it felt smooth and soft to the touch. The liquid's warmth bathed my fingers, some of it traveling down my throat and pooling in my stomach.

I was a model. People paid for high-quality photos of me, all thinking that a curvy woman like myself didn't have any life problems. I had many complications I was still fighting against. The withdrawal effects were beginning to set in again.

Behind me was my sister. The only person I could still trust to get me through this. She was the one that convinced me to leave him behind. My former boyfriend. The guy that ratted me out, telling everyone that I was doing cocaine.

He was misguided, of course. He thought that him telling other people about that would be enough to make me follow the right path, one where there was no cocaine. No white powder on the table before hitting the photograph room and posing for people I'd never meet.

What happened after that was a shitshow.

I had to do everything in my power, pull all my connections, strain my network and do pretty much every other thing I could to make it so my bosses wouldn't think he was telling them the truth.

There was a fallout. I had a heated discussion with him. Kicked his ass out of my life then and there, and he still managed to make me feel bad about it. I cried for days and nights until my sister showed up.

She hugged me then, telling me everything was going to be okay and that, if anything, I was going to be making even more money from now on. Rumors spread, but they were contained and ended up being nothing more than that.

Few people believed them, and it seemed they served to strengthen my reputation. More people joined up my collection of followers on OnlyFans, bought my magazines, looked me up harder on Google and other search platforms, and the like.

Suffice to say that provided me with enough money to pay off this apartment that covered the entirety of the last floor of this hotel. The views from up here of Chicago were stunning. It wasn't as tall as some of the tallest buildings in the city, but vertigo could still strike the mind of some people, if they could get all the way up here and share the apartment with me.

For all my money, I didn't have many friends. My sister was my only friend nowadays, helping me with this and making sure I wouldn't give in to withdrawal. I could feel it clinging to my skin, crawling in my mind, and making the choice of another sniff all too tempting.

But I was stronger than that. I was going to beat it.

My sister approached me, settling her hand on my shoulder and saying, "I'm here for you, always. For whatever you need."

"I know, and thank you, sis," I said, turning my head to her and walking back to the living room. The apartment was nothing short of extravagant, everything built with the highest quality materials, every piece of furniture costing a fortune, and the acoustics of the walls making it impossible to hear any noise from the neighbors.

It was the right kind of place for me.

My life felt empty, though. Without someone to call me his love, a man to kiss me when going out to work, that accepted me for who I was, willing to sacrifice his time and work for me, I just couldn't look at who I was and assume that it was all okay.

There was a very good reason I was taking sleeping pills these last couple of years. And the thought that nothing of this was going to change anytime soon, it saddened me, made me feel more depressed, which sometimes led to irrational assumptions that involved a length of rope and one of the legs of the bed.

There was something funny in the air, wafting in it, and reaching my nose. I sniffed it, my mind in the same instant registering the smell of smoke.

I snapped my head to my sister, saying with a higher tone than normal, "Did you forget the stove on by any chance?"

She widened her eyes, standing up from the couch she was sitting on and putting her hands on her chest.

"No, I didn't forget it on. I was making a chocolate cake, but it's finished. I'm just waiting for it to cool down a little."

"Well, something is burning, and it feels that-"

The interphone chimed in. I rushed to it, sure that if there was a fire blazing in my apartment, that the guy who was supposed to keep all the residents of the hotel happy was going to shout at me. He was going to say I was going to be fined for not taking better care of the apartment and that I should have been more responsible, not letting a fire to start in the building he loved so much.

I pressed the button, the interphone making a louder noise.

"Look, I don't think it's here. I've checked it, and everything is okay in my apartment. It's-"

"Leana, what are you going on about? It's the fire. It's burning the whole building. I don't know how it started, but it's destroying everything, and you need to hit the fire exit as soon as possible. If you don't... I don't want to think about what would happen."

"Wait, what fire?"

"You don't know?"

"No, I don't," I responded, a sense of dread beginning to take root in my heart.

"Look outside your window. I'm not sure if you can see it. From up there, it can be kind of hard," he affirmed, sighing. "I don't know how it happened. One moment everything was fine, and then all the residents started to sprint out of the building, screaming at the top of their lungs."

"Wait, but how? It doesn't make any sense."

"I know, and it doesn't matter. Point is, get the hell out of there as soon as possible. There's a helicopter coming to the building, and it's going to get some people out of here. I don't want to wait for it, though. The police and the fire department are downplaying the scale of the fire for some reason."

"That doesn't make any sense again-" I was shouting, but the connection was cut, nothing more than a sizzling noise coming from within the device.

I whirled around, my eyes looking at my sister.

"There's a fire on the lower levels of the building, and it's spreading. If we don't leave the building right now... I don't want to think about what would happen then."

Depression ate my life from the inside out, but I was still not ready to die. The tempting thoughts involving a length of rope and my bed? Forget them. They were nothing more than delusions from someone who didn't comprehend the finality behind death.

I wanted to live.

"What? What fire?" She asked, tugging at her necklace and hurrying with me over to the balcony. I wasn't one to feel vertigo, but upon settling my fingers on the metal bar and leaning over, I felt as if there was a force pulling me down.

Wind blasted against my face, throwing my hair behind my head.

I didn't know why I was doing this, putting myself at such a risk. I could fall and die, one of the most painful experiences possible defining the last moments of my existence.

Nevertheless, it was worth it to find out if the whole fire thing was nothing more than a ruse or not. And, it was true. My eyes could perceive the smoke and some of the tongues of the blaze slapping against the building, dissolving and eating everything that it touched.

It was moving up like wildfire. People were rushing out of the building, their hands carrying with them as much as they could, and as many suitcases as possible.

I couldn't wrap my head around the fact a fire could begin and spread so fast without first getting notified about it, but it was what was going on. It was no ruse. If I didn't do something now, I was going to be stuck in my apartment waiting for the helicopter to come.

I could see a few blinking lights down on the roads, the noise of extra police vehicles and firetrucks rushing over to Liberty Hotel as fast as possible. There were still not enough of them getting involved to put out the fire and take people out of the building, which was nothing short of puzzling.

Something odd was going on here for sure.

I grabbed my coat, put it on, and said, "We're getting out of here, now."

"Wait, but how?" She asked, sounding more desperate than she needed to be sounding like at this moment. I didn't need the extra stress that came from thinking we might be too late.

"The fire exit. There should be a stair leading all the way to the ground floor, and don't worry, it's covered."

She and I grabbed what we could, certain that the fire was going to be put out before it burned the whole building. That couldn't happen, right? For sure the firefighters were going to sweep right in and put it out with their water hoses and fire extinguishers.

I threw open the door to the hallway, my sister following me from behind, part of me cherishing the fact that I couldn't think of anything else right now. It was all about getting to the ground floor and surviving this.

All about making sure I wouldn't just die and get burned alive in the apartment building.

We opened the fire escape door, took the stairs, and followed them to one of the floors below us. Just as we reached it, we halted, our eyes bulging.

The fire had gotten all the way up here already, and even though it still had a lot of ground to cover until it could blaze my clothes and other belongings in my apartment, it seemed it had already devoured pretty much the whole rest of the building.

I opened the fire escape door that led to the main hallway of this floor, my heart skipping a beat when I noticed the condition it was in. It wasn't just a normal apartment building fire, but one that was bathing the whole structure with its power, dissolving, eating, and ravaging everything it touched.

In front of me, all I could see was the brightness, the flapping of the tongues of the flames, the gush of warmth coming from them, alongside the certainty that I needed to turn on my heels and head to the roof of the building.

But just when the thought crossed my mind, an explosion shook the whole building, making my body topple and get shoved into the blazing hallway, my mouth shooting open and screaming as my eyes closed.

I had one last sight of my sister before finding myself in the blaze's arms, certain that I was going to be burned alive.

At least, unconscious, I wasn't going to scream...

CHAPTER 2

Oliver

I woke up to the sound of the interphone chiming in, rushing to it in nothing but my underwear. I lived a solitary life, without anyone to bother me and judge my choices. Since my wife was burned alive before my very eyes, I couldn't forgive myself, and couldn't think I would ever fall in love again.

I halted in front of the interphone, the sound of the chime annoying me beyond measure. It was the middle of the night, and people should be sleeping and not making calls to me at this moment.

Most people didn't use the interphone to call their neighbors, unless they wished to look like assholes to them. It just might be the case this time, I thought while holding back a chuckle.

It might also be someone in peril, needing to be rescued. I was a firefighter still. I made enough money to pay the rent of this apartment. It wasn't anything special or expensive, and I had just about enough furniture here to live my life with some comfort.

I could feel waves of heat coming from the door, and I couldn't help but suspect that something was burning in the hallway. The room was safe from whatever was going on there, for the most part. If a bunch of little kids had put fire on something in the main corridor, then it wasn't going to take much longer for the sprinklers to kick in and cut their fun short.

I pressed the big call button of the interphone, a familiar and irritating voice announcing its presence.

"Oliver, are you there?"

"Yeah, I'm here."

He was the supervisor of the building, and he sounded breathless, like he'd been running for hours before getting to the interphone and deciding he needed to talk to me.

"There's a fire burning the whole building. You need to get out of your room, now."

"Huh? Right now? What are you talking about?" I questioned, still feeling the waves of heat coming from behind the doorway that led to the main hallway, my ears finding it strange there was an absence of kid noises in the air. If they were out there, then they should be running in the corridor, jumping and giggling, and doing other mischievous things.

Something odd was going on here for sure, and I needed to find the truth behind it.

"Just go to the balcony and you'll see what I'm talking about. I'm still in the building, and there are some firemen and the local police working to get everyone out. But, the fire is spreading too fast, and I fear it's already devouring your floor, too."

"What the hell–" I uttered when the connection was lost, a sizzling noise following suit as an explosion shook the whole building. I thought it was going to be toppled over, killing not just me, but all the residents still inside it. However, that didn't come to pass.

I stumbled as I made a beeline to the balcony, gripping the bars of the short wall made of glass and metal, and turning my head to look down.

There it was. The aforementioned blaze, burning and devouring everything in its path. There weren't just the local police and firetrucks in the vicinity, but also news channel helicopters, drones, and neighbors from other buildings and houses doing what they could to help to put out the fire.

As a fireman who thought I wouldn't have to work tonight, seeing what I was witnessing terrified me. Thoughts of my dear late wife dying in front of me, in my arms, flashed across my mind.

I was still not sure I wanted to keep working as a fireman, even though, at the moment, it seemed I didn't have much of a choice.

It was either putting into practice everything I'd learned, or succumbing to the fire alongside the rest of the residents that couldn't get out.

I needed to do something, and fast.

I whirled around when another explosion shook the whole place, the hinges of the door getting broken by an excessive force, followed by none other than a woman coming through the now empty doorway, stumbling and losing her balance soon after.

Her legs collided against one of the couches of the living room, and she fell on her backside on the carpet, eyes sealed.

She'd lost her consciousness, and seeing her like that kicked in something feral and unrelenting in me. I didn't know who she was, but I was going to do everything in my power to get her out of here, and safe.

Spread on the floor, whole body and clothes dirtied by the dust of the explosion, it was clear she needed a fireman to save her from this imminent danger. And I was the only one that could pull that off.

She was just one of the many residents in peril, running away from the fire, begging for a man to become her guardian angel. I was so sure of that the first thing I did was to rush straight to her and hold her torso in my arms.

I lifted it gently, for I knew an explosion had just hit her and sent her stumbling into my room. Whoever this woman was, whose smooth skin begged for my hands to touch it, she needed me.

Now, more than ever before, she needed a fireman to save her.

I studied her body with my eyes for some moments, noticing the fire burning the walls and everything else in the main corridor. I was sleeping through the whole night. I didn't smell any smoke sneaking into my room, and most of all, I didn't think a fire would spread so fast in a building as populated as this one without people first noticing that.

If it were an accident, that was. One could never rule out the possibility that it had been premeditated.

She was a bigger girl, of the kind that didn't feel ashamed of herself. She had on a pair of jeans and a red blouse. And the color and the tone of her hair, blond and shiny, despite the dirt that was spilled all over, tantalized me.

Her eyes were closed. I wished I could see them now, though that was just me being selfish. Her chest expanded and contracted, showing me she was still alive. I sighed in relief. If she were dead, I didn't think I would have forgiven myself.

I didn't know why, but she did remind me of my former wife a little, which in turn kicked in the need to prevent the same that happened that night from occurring again with her.

I couldn't let that come to pass. I'd do anything to keep this woman safe, even though I still had no idea who she was, other than the fact we shared the same apartment building.

Her lips looked full and plump. They made me want to kiss them right at this moment. It would be a kiss that would wake her, her eyes opening, and then she'd tell me she was thankful I was the one that showed up to get her out of danger.

I caressed her forehead, pushing a lock of her hair to the side and tucking it behind her ear. Her eyes threatened to open. My whole body froze, unsure what I'd be telling her when she was awake and perceived me.

She was going to wonder what the hell I was doing, holding her like this without her permission, with no chance in hell this would be happening if it weren't for the unusual circumstances we found ourselves in.

Most of all, something needed to be done about the fire burning everything outside and that was already creeping into the room. If we stayed here for too long, we weren't going to have any chance of escape.

And, at this moment, there was only one way to get out. An issue prevented me from making that possible, though. I was going to have to bust out my hatchet and make a hole in one of the halls – the blaze was eating up the whole hallway. From there, we were going to have to proceed to the floor under us, and hope that the fire hadn't already consumed everything there, too.

From the looks of things, the fire destroying everything in its path, it seemed we might not get the luck we needed.

Her eyelids fluttered open, the pupils of her eyes meeting mine, something indescribable flashing in them for nothing more than a moment. I wished to ask her what that was, but I was frozen in place, the realization that this was happening, that I was going to have to save her no matter the cost, sinking in.

I couldn't let the same that happened to my wife come to pass with her. *It won't.*

I helped her to stand up, her hands dusting off the dirt and the minuscule debris on her body. Her eyes turned to the right, finding the blaze eating up the main hallway as she came to the conclusion I'd encountered before – we couldn't get out, no through there anyway.

"We need to get out of here. I'm going to open up a hole in one of the walls, and from there we are going to try to get to the emergency stairs. It's the only way out of here."

"Oh, hey," she said while sounding and looking dizzy, like she wasn't quite here with me. "My name is Leana. If we are going to be working together now to get out–"

Her eyes closed, her body swaying, and I knew what was happening before she could mutter another word about it. I swooped in, holding her in my arms, my eyes locking with her.

"You've been through a lot. You don't need to say anything else."

Not only was she going through a lot right now, but it also seemed there was something in her past that had been plaguing her mind. I wished I could ask her about that, and in other circumstances, I'd be doing that, but the moment didn't allow me to be the gentleman I knew I could be. I needed to be the firefighter I'd always been.

Such a beauty, such a flower didn't deserve to be going through this kind of hardship.

Getting a grip of herself, she stumbled away from me and said, "No, it's okay. I can keep going. I can help."

"You're not going to tell me who you are?" I asked, smirking.

I knew her name was Leana, but I'd like to hear it again, coming through those beautiful and rosy lips of hers. She hadn't worn lipstick tonight, which was pretty telling. She hadn't suspected the apartment building was going to be burning down like this.

She raised one of her eyebrows, but still answered my question.

"It's Leana, and I think we should make the introductions as quick as possible. The fire is getting here, too. I don't know about you, but I don't want to die."

The atmosphere was beginning to grow livelier and less gloomy, thanks to her apparent personality and the way she spoke. I wished I could make the most of that, get to know her better, but right now, we were stuck here and we could die if we didn't plan our escape well.

There was the emergency exit, the stairs that led to the ground floor, and they were our only chance to get out of here in one piece.

"Right, of course. I'm Oliver, and I'm a firefighter."

"If you are one, then shouldn't you be down there putting out the fire with the rest of your crew?" She asked, cocking her head.

"No, I thought that tonight I wouldn't have to work. I'm actually looking to get a new job elsewhere, something different that doesn't remind me of fires all the time."

"Huh? Are you hiding something from me I should know about?"

I shook my head, not wishing to tell a stranger anything about my past life. It hurt me too much, just thinking about it wringing my heart a little now. Some time had already passed since then, but it still felt like it occurred just a couple of days ago.

Most of all, I needed to make use of this opportunity to not think about my former wife.

Leana was a stunning girl. Younger than me – much, much so – but still such an out-of-this-world beauty that she made me wish I could get to know her better.

It was such a pity that we were meeting in such strenuous circumstances.

Well, no point in letting those thoughts consume my mind. I need to make a hole in the wall between my apartment and that of my neighbor, and then find a way to sneak to the emergency exit stairs.

It was the only way to get out of here.

CHAPTER 3

Leana

When the explosion happened, blasting me into his room, I didn't think I'd come across such a stunning man. He was a hulking specimen, muscles on top of muscles, broad shoulders, and a wide chest that had made my pussy throb when he was holding me in his arms.

I wished he could do that again, but I wasn't going to push my luck, either.

He'd been trying for half an hour now, attempting to carve a hole in another wall, which was the last one leading to the emergency exit. I'd told him chances were the rest of the stairs had also been blocked by the fire and the multiple, small explosions that shook the building, but he didn't want to listen to me.

He was a protector, the kind of man willing to put his life at risk to keep others safe. When he noticed me, saw me for the first time lying on the carpet of his living room, something different flashed across his eyes, and I wished he could tell me what that was.

But he was determined not to talk to me, hitting the wall in front of him over and over again with his hatchet, his muscles bulging, his presence growing by the second.

Sweat was pooling all over his body, his veins bulging out.

I couldn't take anymore what I was seeing, so I settled my hand on his shoulder. He spun around in a fraction of a second, eyes meeting mine, making me fear he was going to hit me or do something worse.

But he didn't, just sighing and dropping his hatchet. It fell over on the ground with a thud as he proceeded to the balcony of his neighbor's apartment.

We were trapped in here now, and I couldn't help but think this was the right opportunity I'd been seeking since meeting him. His dark blue eyes spoke of his past, of his former life, and I wished he could tell me a little about it.

Maybe I was just being selfish, but I felt like I needed him to tell me what had happened before in his life. I could see the burden in his body posture, his lack of words for me, and how he carried himself.

There was a deep wound in his past he wasn't willing to tell me about, but why?

I stood slightly behind him, to his side, putting my hand on my chest.

"Oliver... it's okay. We are going to find a way to get to the roof."

"I know... I just don't want to think I might fail you."

"You're not failing me. Nobody knew about the fire until it was too late."

"I'm a firefighter. I'm supposed to save people like you."

"You already are," I said, proceeding to him. "I think there's something that's troubling you and that you're hiding from me."

He shook his head.

"I'm not hiding anything."

I couldn't give up on finding out more about him, even though he was nothing more than a stranger. I felt like I knew this man, that I could understand the rest of him and coerce him to tell me everything I wanted to know about his wound.

A man of his kind, tall and so imponent, looking hurt like this, had to be hiding something from me.

"Look, you can tell me. I'd never tell anyone about it. I'm the kind of woman that can keep secrets safe," I argued, quirking up a corner of my lips.

He sighed. There was a moment of silence. I turned around and proceeded away from him. Someone like him needed time, and I wasn't going to force anything on him.

Outside the room, the flames were still eating up everything, devouring the walls. My eyes could notice some helicopters coming this way. They were going to get us out of here for sure. More firetrucks populated the roads down below, using their ladders and water hoses to help to put out the fire.

But it was a lost cause. Whatever happened, if someone set the building ablaze, then they knew what they were doing. And if they did, they were also long gone from here, running to the nearest airport and heading to a country where the USA had no power over.

We'd been talking before about how to get out of this building and sharing some of what we could of our lives, but he still hadn't told me anything meaty about his past. I wished he'd do that and prove to me he was a better man than I thought he was.

"There's something about me you need to know," he finally said, exhaling.

My heart skipped a beat. Was Oliver going to reveal what he'd been keeping buried in his mind this whole time? I was aware that not a lot of time had passed between us yet, but since getting to know him and spending these precious minutes with him, I could feel a connection between me and him forming.

It was as if meeting him was showing me that things could be better in my life, that I could find someone worth loving again.

"My wife died in a house fire. Our house. I couldn't keep her safe. I knew everything. I knew the house like the back of my hand, but when it mattered the most, I couldn't keep the only person I loved safe."

His bottom lip trembled, but he didn't cry. No tears came out. I couldn't help but feel a deeper connection with him, wishing he could tell me more about what he'd just mentioned.

His wife was killed by a fire? No wonder the current situation was troubling him.

"I'm not going to die here," I insisted, proceeding to him and grabbing his hand. "I have someone willing to go above and beyond to keep me alive."

"It's not that simple. If I failed once, I can fail again. And if we don't get to the roof and the rescue helicopters, this whole building is going to collapse and bury us."

His eyes meeting mine, I could tell once again how much that story of his was disturbing his mind. He was remembering every single detail of what came to pass then, thinking he was helpless and couldn't do anything to get us out of this tight spot.

I squeezed his hand, saying, "Well, no point in feeling that way and letting those thoughts consume your mind. There's something I wish to tell you, if you're willing to listen."

"What kind of thing?" He asked, turning and standing in front of me.

Seeing him like this, in front of me, made me forget about the fire tongues slapping against the walls outside in the hallway, consuming everything, threatening to end our lives the most horrible way possible.

"I'm a model."

"You are? Then, you were probably living on one of the top floors. They are pretty expensive."

"I was, and that is a little beside the point now," I said, grabbing his other hand, feeling how callous they were. The hands of a true firefighter, one willing to put his life at risk to save others.

He didn't need to be bringing me with him now, but here he was, doing just that.

"Then, what are you waiting for? Don't keep me hanging here," he insisted, leaning over to me, threatening to kiss me now, despite all the pain the outcome of that might wash him over with.

"The point is that I'd thought I'd never meet a man like you ever again in my life. I've been meeting so many assholes, guys thinking they needed a piece of me, nothing more than a one-night stand, and then pretend they didn't even know me. That kind of thing hurt, and I'm glad it's long gone now."

"What do you mean?" He asked, leaning down some more, putting his arms behind my back, pulling me to him. The heat coming from underneath and behind us reminded me that the flames were still very much alive, of how we needed to get out of here as soon as possible. But I couldn't worry about those things when this stud was so willing to kiss me now.

After everything that happened, he was opening up to me and showing me the kind of man he was.

"I had a boyfriend once, and he was such an asshole-"

"Well, if I find that man, I'm going to whoop his ass."

"I know you will, but let me finish first."

"Alright," he joked, kissing my lips, sending shockwaves of pleasure through my whole body.

I smiled without showing my teeth, saying, "He ratted me out once, telling everyone I knew that I did cocaine."

"And did you, or was he lying?" He asked, widening his eyes.

Despite knowing that now, he kept his posture straight and didn't step away from me. There was something about all this that kept telling him he needed to hear me out, that it was worth it.

It was an instantaneous, deep connection no one could ever break. This firefighter was falling in love with me, and there was no denying that.

"I used to sniff cocaine every day, yes," I responded, lowering my head in shame. It wasn't something I liked to admit, but with him standing in front of me this way, his eyes judging me, his warmth comforting me despite the heat coming in waves from the rest of the building... It was an addictive moment. I could remain like this forever, if it wasn't for the fact we needed to get out here before the fire consumed us.

His hand cupped my chin, tilting my head up, eyes locking with mine, something wild running across in them.

"I don't know what happened, but if that makes you feel depressed, then know it's nothing more than a silly thing. It's over now, right? You're not a drug addict anymore."

"No, I'm not... but that thing, what he did, it made me feel like never falling in love again. I've always thought all men are assholes since then."

His hand caressed my cheek, reminding me of his presence, stepping toward me some more, showing me that despite my curvier frame, I was small compared to him.

This was a silly thing to be doing. This whole thing didn't make any sense. I'd never felt such a strong connection to someone before. Here he was, nothing more than a fireman, putting his arms around me and letting me hug him.

I hugged him, embraced this firefighter, making him mine and crying on his chest at the same time. Sobbing was all I could do, the tears streaking down my cheeks. I could remain like this forever. There was no denying this was the first case of love at first sight in my life, and I couldn't keep it contained any longer.

I was in love with this man, this firefighter, and he was kissing me now, too.

"We have some time, so might as well," he cooed, obsessing over me and pushing me toward the bed.

I was crying, there was a curriculum of thoughts surging in my mind, and I was still convincing myself we were doing the right thing.

If we were going to die alive and burned to a crisp, then we might as well make the most of it. One fuck before succumbing to death.

CHAPTER 4

Oliver

It didn't make much sense. I was supposed to be doing everything in my power to get her out of here. If not for me, then I was supposed to be doing that just for her. I wasn't supposed to be falling in love with a stranger, even though everything and every bone in my body were telling me we were doing the right thing.

Her hands flew in the air, an aura of desperation around them, pulling down the zipper of my pants. She wanted this, and she needed a man like me in her life. Leana, the woman I never thought I'd fall in love with. She was a model. She was rich as fuck.

As for me, I was nothing more than a fool who thought I'd amount to something one day. And yet, here I was, bonding with her and making love with her. The heat coming from all over the rest of the building pulsed to us, making this moment hotter than it needed to be, and it reminded me of all the times I loved my late life.

I kissed her, connecting my lips with hers, sealing our tongues together, and letting the battle ensue. I took control of her mouth, rubbing my lips against hers, closing my eyes, and letting the significance of this moment bathe me with it.

It didn't matter what had happened before. It mattered what was happening in the here and now.

Her hands fought against my pants, pushing them down. Grinding my hips and groin against her, I made her moan, which in turn stiffened my dick that much more. The heat of this moment was bathing me with it, the seconds ticking by and making me surer that I needed to get inside her as soon as possible.

I pushed my pants all the way down, kicking them away. She traced my thighs with her hands, cupping my balls, my bulge, and then squeezing it for a second before erupting into a round of giggles.

It took me no time to take off my underwear, tossing it all the way over to the flames. I worried that, if we were to survive this, that I'd have to be walking around without a pair on, but it was alright. I guessed that it didn't matter much.

I loved her curves, kissing her, ripping her blouse open, unsnapping her bra, and finally reaching the promised land that was her pair of naked boobs. I pinched her nipples, making her moan and groan, Leana closing her eyes.

Kissing her some more, I left various hickeys all over her skin she was never going to forget. I didn't know if I was going to come out of this alive. Maybe I was already looking at it as some kind of honorable death I needed to end my torment of thoughts, but the truth was that at this moment just one thing mattered to me – making Leana the happiest woman in the whole world.

I was going to prove to her there was nothing to be afraid of, that she didn't need to be thinking all the time that all men were like her ex-boyfriend. He might have thought he was doing the right thing then, but he was just being an asshole. Who the hell went around telling other people his girlfriend was doing drugs?

I kissed her some more, proceeding to her lower abdomen, the bed creaking while flaming tongues slapped against the wall of the room behind the bed. She didn't attempt to stop me, rather giving herself fully for me, allowing me to rip off her pair of lacy panties.

Funny thing that was. She was also going to have to be walking around without her underwear on once this whole thing was over. Reaffirming my compromise, I told her multiple times I was going to get her out of here, out of this burning room, one way or another.

Leana squirmed, telling me to give her some seconds to breathe, but I just couldn't. I kept groping her whole body, kissing her nipples, her boobs, hardening the skin of her little rosebud, only halting when the wildest thought crossed my mind.

I didn't have a condom with me. Didn't think that tonight I was going to have sex. Not with such a stunning, eye-catchy beauty.

Meanwhile, all Leana could do was to keep digging her fingers into my shirt, into my skin, assessing me for the kind of man I was, who just might be a little too big for her. I didn't let that sort of consideration ruin the mood we were setting in here, still kissing her some more, roaming her body, cherishing each of her curves.

"Please, just get inside me," she murmured.

"Are you on your pill?" I asked, stopping just for a couple of seconds to give her a moment to breathe.

"No, of course not. I didn't think I would be dating such a stunning man tonight."

"Well, me neither," I said, kissing her little rosebud, flicking my tongue and making her whole body shudder. Leana was so willing, most likely not thinking like the rational woman she was most of the time.

"Then, don't let that stop you."

"Are you sure?" I asked, still kissing her belly, and then moving down and licking her folds. I was getting her ready, more than prepared for the kind of entry I was going to make her endure. She was going to take all of me inside her, and then she was going to be begging for more.

"Yes, I'm sure," she assured me, and that was everything I needed before easing myself in her, feeling her walls tightening around me.

I wasn't thinking like the rational firefighter I was supposed to be as well. I was making love with a model when I was supposed to be opening up a hole in that wall and escaping from this blazing room...

CHAPTER 5

Leana

I guessed this whole thing was always going to be happening one day. Me giving myself fully for another man. I was being silly when I thought all other men were like my former boyfriend. Oliver was someone else, another man, of a different breed.

And he was obsessed with me.

"Please, just get inside me. I don't care if you're going to make me pregnant or not. Might as well, right, since the whole building is going to come crashing down on our heads."

"Aye, might as well," he purred, easing his big prick into my fanny, ending me then and there.

Pleasure kept building up inside me, like water in a dam's large reservoir. Like that, except there was no end to it. The more he kept doing it, adding more of his inches inside me, the closer I felt to reaching my orgasm.

And with me being the kind of woman I was, I could climax multiple times tonight, not worrying at all about the fire that was going to come and eat us up.

He got in all the way, reaching the end of my tunnel, stopping for a moment to assess the occasion. It didn't matter to him if the blaze was going to kill him or not – he was making sure he was teaching me one valuable lesson tonight, that there were still men like him.

Gentlemen. Men willing to put their lives at risk for strangers they loved, like me.

His thrusts were slow and measured at the beginning, measured even. He wanted to make sure he wasn't going to hurt me now, turn this into one of the most promising and unforgettable moments of my life.

As for me, I couldn't help but keep meeting his pounds, thrust for thrust. His balls slapped against my ass, ever so gently, sweat pooling all over the skin of his naked, study body.

His muscles tensed and eased up, bulging, relaxing as he worked me with all his might, always keeping himself inside me. Oliver stretched me all the way, as wide as possible, always sliding almost without friction.

He was fucking me, making love with me, and I couldn't help but throw my head back and let out a long, guttural moan escape my lips. I'd been keeping it at bay this whole time, waiting for the right moment to come.

And said moment came, my whole body shuddering, covering his cock with my cunt's juices. He kept pounding my rump with all his might, balls slapping against my buttocks wildly, the sounds of slapping filling the room.

I couldn't even hear the sound of the helicopters flying over the building, picking up people and getting them to safety. Were we going to get out of here with them? I didn't know and didn't care, the ecstasy of this moment filling me with joy, lust, and pleasure.

My whole body shook one more time, toes curling, still meeting his thrust, one pound for another pound, willing him to ease even more of his inches inside me.

I just couldn't have enough of him.

His dick erupted all of a sudden, and he didn't even warn me. I didn't know if I was going to get pregnant from this, but I also supposed it didn't matter. I was going to die here anyway, engulfed by the growing flames.

His cream was milky and thick, viscous even, taking a while to coat the entirety of my inside walls. And when I thought that was going to be the sign he needed to pull out and lie down on the bed, he did the unthinkable, still fucking me and making love with me.

Fucking hell, I loved how unrelenting Oliver was. I hadn't had a fuck like this in a very, very long time, and if I survived this, I was going to have a long and wild story to tell my sister.

And also the rest of my family, but they were bygone thoughts.

His dick kept twitching, pumping out more of his sperm, filling me so much it was leaking out. Dammit, I didn't want any of it coming out. I wanted it all inside me, so I tightened the grip of my pussy around his rod, milking even more of his seeds, making sure his shaft was going to remain inside me for the rest of the night.

When he finished, his body shuddered, but Oliver didn't pull out. Rather, he stayed inside me, his eyes locking with mine one more time, lips connecting for another powerful kiss.

"I love you, Leana. I want you to know that," he murmured, nibbling my earlobe.

"I know," I said. "And I love you too. Marry me?"

He chuckled. "In the middle of the fire, you're asking to marry me? You're sure that's something you want to make happen, miss?"

"Yes, I'm sure. There's only one man I want in my life, and he's you."

"But I'm nothing more than a stranger, your one-night stand. Even if we survive this–"

"We are going to get out of this building, love. I'm going to find a way."

"You're going to find a way?"

I narrowed my eyes a little, judging him. "So, are you going to marry me or not?"

"A bit too early to be talking about that kind of thing, but yeah, I want to marry you. You're the love of my life as well. I've been thinking about asking you the same, in fact."

Oliver didn't pull out, lying down and turning me until I was facing him.

"Let's do it one more time?" I asked of him, urging him to make this moment even more memorable.

"Sure, but just one more time."

CHAPTER 6

Oliver

By luck and persistence more than anything, we managed to get out of that room. I opened up another hole in the wall. I didn't know what got into me, but after having sex with Leana, I felt reinvigorated. I felt as if I could take on the whole world, and win.

We slipped out into the burning hallway, holding Leana in my arms. I took her up the stairs and came across a shadow rounding the corner of another corridor. It was another woman that looked just like Leana. The resemblance was uncanny.

I halted, for a moment a layer of silence dawning on us, the flames slapping the walls of the rooms and threatening to burn us to a crisp. Sweat was layering the skin of my body, and I couldn't help but notice all the dirt and the ash covering our bodies.

This was a tough night, one I was never going to forget.

Still holding Leana in my arms, I felt that I could take her all the way to the roof. She'd mentioned she could walk just fine, but I was persistent. She was my Queen, and as a part of the realty, she deserved to be carried around by me.

She shouldn't walk. She didn't need to. If it came to that, I'd stroll with her in my arms and cross the whole world. I'd make a dream of hers come true – the one that involved visiting every country in existence.

"Leana! Oh, I'm so, so sorry. I thought I wasn't going to find you again," the stranger said, widening her eyes.

"Sis! I couldn't find you as well, and I was trapped in a room. It was thanks to Oliver here that we managed to get out."

"His name is Oliver?" She asked, raking me over with her eyes, the lust in her pupils nothing short of perceptible. "I'm glad there was still someone in here willing to help you. Everyone that couldn't manage to get to the ground floor is getting carried by the helicopters, and we can't miss our chance. If they think there's no one else here–"

"We'll get left behind. Don't worry, I'm not going to let that happen," I promised, stepping to her and heading to the last flight of stairs. "We don't have any time to waste."

I pushed past her, the only concern in my mind the one that involved getting to the roof of the building and putting Leana in one of the helicopters. It didn't matter if they were going to have enough space for me as well – all that was of importance was getting her out of here, away from those dancing flames.

"And I guess there's also no time for introductions," her sister complained, but I ignored her. I wasn't an ass, I just didn't want to waste time with handshakes.

We battled against various obstacles, ruined doors, crumbling walls, and other kinds of dangers. Throwing open one more door, we at long last reached the roof, the violent wind kissing my cheeks, throwing her hair in different and wild directions.

I tilted my head down, looking at her. "We've made it."

"I know," she said, pulling herself up and kissing my lips.

I couldn't wait to get home.

EPILOGUE

Leana

The decoration was nothing short of breathtaking. After living for so many years in an apartment, I was digging what the future held in store for me. Living in a big, two-story house in a closed-gate community. In here, we were going to have all the safety and good neighbors we needed.

Even the weather was helping to make my dream come true. Cyan sky, snow-white clouds, no sign of any rain bathing this region any time soon, the birds tweeting in the trees, and some neighbors already coming out of their homes and greeting us.

There was nothing like your typical American dream, away from any debts, people willing to fuck me up, and having to fake emotions in front of a camera.

And no, don't worry. That doesn't mean I decided to quit. I still worked as a model, but now I looked at it with different eyes. I could go there for work, let the fine men behind their big cameras take photos of me, upload them to the internet and then proclaim me as the most attractive curvier girl in the whole country.

It all worked for me, making me feel more and more fulfilled, the thought that there was nothing I'd rather be doing with my life completing me beyond measure.

I turned around when he opened the door, proceeding to me and settling his hands on my belly. It wasn't growing or anything, so I was getting surer I wasn't pregnant. Guess I could go to a hospital and get it checked, but I also couldn't find the time for that, and I didn't feel like supporting the repulsive American health system any more than I already did.

Plus, it didn't change anything. When I was ready for a baby, we were going to try for it. I could just imagine him or her running around, making friends, smiling, and giggling all the time. There was a layer of tantalization around that, no doubt about it, but the coming months didn't ask for that sort of thing.

Rather, they asked for something that couldn't be mentioned.

It was the middle of the day, but his cock, straining against my buttocks, was asking for that.

I giggled. "Oliver, you're making me blush. The neighbors are all going to pucker their noses at us and stop giving us cookies on Sundays."

"Let them think whatever they want of us. All I know is that I'm not going to feel embarrassed because of some prudes."

"But they are our neighbors and all. We should be more respectful of them."

He took a step backward, taking me with him and leading me back into the house.

I made him stop, some of the neighbors throwing accusatory looks at us. "They are already catching a whiff of this."

"What did I say about neighbors and privacy? They have nothing to complain about. They all know we have sexy time at home."

"Yes, but in there, not out here," I complained, getting a smile from his stubbly and chiseled face.

"That's why I'm taking us there," he said, proceeding to the door, back turned to it, and then closing it once we were in the living room. He kicked it close with his right foot, and while I didn't like that one bit, I couldn't complain about it.

I was far too immersed in what he was making me feel, his hands groping my body, making me feel like a woman again. Oliver knew how to push all the right buttons. Breaths of air were coming out through my semi-open mouth, making my skin ooze sweat.

This was a hot Spring day, but not warm enough to be making me sweat this much.

Oliver was taking off his clothes before I could even ask what was going on here, his hands pushing down his jeans and pressing his cock harder against me. He allowed me to cherish the tension of his balls on my ass, and I couldn't help but look for them with my hand, cupping them.

"Hmm, who's the naughty one now?" He asked, grinding his body against mine.

I could already feel the smell of his pre-cum wafting in the air, and it was reminding me of his presence, of his manliness, and of the position of power he held over me. In contrast, I controlled his thoughts too, but not to such an extent.

He was asserting his dominance, showing me he was always going to be here, right beside me, when I needed him.

"I'm not naughty. I'm just following the rhythm."

"Oh, right. *Just following the rhythm.* Nothing more than that?"

"No, nothing more than that," I said, turning around and kissing him, before he could do anything else.

He broke the kiss, his smoldering eyes burning me with their unrelenting intensity. I dared to look down, finding the silhouette of his cock oozing out his pre-cum, and it was making me wonder if now wouldn't be the right time to try for a baby with him.

Living in a two-story house was nice and all, but there was something about having another life with us, sharing this environment, that I couldn't quite put into words. Suffice to say I needed to make it happen, no matter the cost.

No matter if it took away our freedom and privacy.

Still feeling his cock pressing against my groin region, I couldn't help but undo the belt of my pants, push it down, and rip off my panties. Dammit, I guessed I was going to have to buy a new pair tomorrow.

Well, it didn't matter now. Here I was, seeing his big, fat cock in front of me one more time, the temptation to just wrap my lips around it a bit too urging for my heart, making it speed up like nothing before it could.

I did just that, getting on my knees, the sounds of the tweeting birds outside reminding me we were living a life many people were still seeking.

As for Oliver here... He still worked as a firefighter. He couldn't drop his profession, so he was still working as one of the men people loved seeing doing his thing.

His gland was nothing short of enormous, making me stretch my lips all the way, covering it with them. I bobbed up and down on him, and cupped his balls in my hand, playing with them, teasing them, and tugging them ever so slightly to remind him of the position of power I held over him.

"Fuck me, fuck me," he muttered, not wishing to cum right now and end all the fun. For Mr. Fireman here, this could go on and on forever, until there was nothing left of me.

Heat was rising in me, bubbling, with my orgasm building up and threatening to wash over me. I needed that. I needed those things reminding me of how good I had it here, and I would never let anyone tell me otherwise.

His balls were beginning to get hotter. His moans, filling the room. For sure some of the neighbors were already hearing this, but it didn't matter. I couldn't care about that right now.

I was still bobbing up and down his length, feeling the veins bulging out, more of his pre-cum oozing and gracing my tongue with its presence, his balls touching my chin now because I was deep throating Oliver.

And just when I thought he was going to erupt inside my mouth, ending this whole thing before he had the chance to make me pregnant, he grabbed a fistful of my hair and pulled my head backward.

"Sorry, Leana, but there's only one place where it's going now," he growled, sweeping me up in his arms and carrying me all the way to our bed, his cock bouncing up and down as he did that.

He pushed me down on the bed, spreading me on it, and then eased his big prick without asking for my permission. It was a silly thing, but he didn't do it.

His cock pressed against my walls, widening them all the way, making a surge of pain roam free through my body.

I screamed a little, but not enough to bother any of the neighbors. I just loved the direction this was taking, becoming one with the firefighter, melding our lives together. He was going to make a baby of his in me, and I was going to be one of the happiest women in the whole world.

I knew he or she was going to change our lives forever.

The End

Thank you for the reception for my previous books. Writing BBW Alpha Male is something that always excites me, and it's so great to know there's a whole audience hungry for that kind of story.

As one last little thing, I'd like to request you to leave a review for this book on the Amazon store page (or just how many stars you think it deserves). It doesn't take long, and your opinion is very valuable to me. I know some of you leave your reviews on Goodreads, but on Amazon is where they have more visibility, and you'd be helping me a lot, too.

OTHER BOOKS BY JOLIE DAMMAN

Snowy Curves: A BBW Alpha Male Romance
Christmas Curves: A BBW Alpha Male Romance
Venom Curves: A BBW Alpha Male Romance
Impossibly Curvy: A BBW Alpha Male
Wild Curves: A Western BBW Alpha Male Instalove Romance
Unfair Curves: A BBW Alpha Male Romance Bundle
Mafia Vassal: A Dark Italian Mafia Romance Bundle
Beg Me: An Arranged Marriage Dark Mafia Romance
Don't Cry: A Secret Baby Dark Mafia Romance
Seizing her Heart: A Bratva Mafia Romance Collection
Conquering my Queen: A Dark Mafia Romance Bundle
Challenging Destiny: An Arranged Marriage Dark Mafia Romance
Chaining my Queen: A Secret Baby Dark Mafia Romance
Hell is Crying: A Secret Baby Mafia Romance
Beyond Forgiving: A Dark Mafia Captive Romance
Chosen to be Mine: A Dark Arranged Marriage Mafia Romance
Have no Fear: An Enemies to Lovers Academy Romance
Under his Mercy: A Dark High School Bully Romance
Lure Me: A Dark High School Bully Romance
Fallen Angel: A Dark High School Bully Romance
Stop Lying: A Dark High School and College Bundle
Stop Running: A Dark High School Bully Romance
Take Control: A Dark High School Bully Romance

ABOUT THE AUTHOR

Jolie Damman lives with her puppies and many cats on her farmland. She enjoys spending time with nature and tending to her property. When she has some free time, which doesn't happen as often as she would like, she writes her books.

As a writer, she hopes to touch and change the heart of her readers. Her books are not for those weak of the heart, and they tend to be spicier than most. One word after the other, she doesn't stop typing until she has written her idea, and she is very desire-driven when it comes to establishing the connections of her characters.

www.ingramcontent.com/pod-product-compliance
Lightning Source LLC
Chambersburg PA
CBHW060928130726
48001CB00006B/2471